THE
PENTECOST OF
CALAMITY

By
OWEN WISTER
Author of " The Virginian," etc.

New York
THE MACMILLAN COMPANY
1916

Norwood Press
J. S. Cushing Co. — Berwick & Smith Co.
Norwood, Mass., U.S.A.

I

THE PENTECOST OF CALAMITY

Ever the fiery Pentecost
Girds with one flame the countless host.
— EMERSON.

I

BY various influences and agents the Past is summoned before us, more vivid than a dream. The process seems as magical as those whereof we read in fairy legends, where circles are drawn, wands waved, mystic syllables pronounced. Adjured by these rites, voices speak, or forms and faces shape themselves from nothing. So, through certain influences, not magical at all, our brains are made to flash with visions

of other days. Is there among us one
to whom this experience is unknown?
For whom no particular strain of music,
or no special perfume, is linked with
an inveterate association? Music and
perfumes are among the most potent
of these evocatory agents; but many
more exist, such as words, sounds, hand-
writing. Thus almost always, at the
name of the town Cologne, the banks
of the golden stream, the German
Rhine, sweep into my sight as first I
saw them long ago; and from a steamer's
deck I watch again, and again count, a
train composed of twenty-one locomotives, moving ominous and sinister on
their new errand. That was July 19,
1870. France had declared war on
Prussia that day. Mobilization was beginning before my eyes. I was ten.

Dates and anniversaries also perform the same office as music and perfumes. This is the ninth of June. This day, last year, I was in the heart of Germany. The beautiful, peaceful scene is plain yet. It seems as if I never could forget it or cease to love it. Often last June I thought how different the sights I was then seeing were from those twenty-one locomotives rolling their heavy threat along the banks of the Rhine. And, for the mere curiosity of it, I looked in my German diary to find if I had recorded anything on last June ninth that should be worth repeating on this June ninth.

Well, at the end of the day's jotted routine were the following sentences: "I am constantly more impressed with the Germans. They are a massive, ongoing, steady race. Some unifying slow fire is at work in them. This can be felt, somehow." Such was my American impression, innocent altogether, deeply innocent, and ignorant of what the slow fire was going to become. So were the peasants and the other humbler subjects of the Empire who gave me this daily impression; they were innocent and ignorant too. Therefore is the German tragedy deeper even than the Belgian.

On June twenty-eighth I was still in the heart of Germany, but at another beautiful place, where further signs of Germany's great thrift, order and competence had met me at every turn. It was a Sunday, cloudless and hot, with the mountains full of odors from the pines. After two hours of strolling I reëntered our hotel to find a group of travelers before the bulletin board. Here we read in silence the news of a political assassination. The silence was prolonged, not because this news touched any of us nationally but because any such crime must touch and shock all thoughtful persons.

At last the silence was broken by an old German traveler, who said: "That is the match which will set all Europe in a blaze." We did not know who he was. None of our party ever knew. On the next morning this party took its untroubled way toward France, a party of innocent, ignorant Americans, in whose minds lingered no thought of the old German's remark. That evening we slept in Rheims. Our windows opened opposite the quiet cathedral.

It towered far above them into the night and sky, its presence filling our rooms with a serene and grave benediction. Just to see it from one's pillow gave to one's thoughts the quality of prayer.

Two days later I took my leave of it by sitting for a silent hour alone beneath its solemn nave. I can never be too glad that I bade it this good-by. Not long afterward — only thirty-two days — we recollected the old German's remark, for suddenly it came true. He had known whereof he spoke. On August 1, 1914, Europe fell to pieces; and during August, 1915, in a few weeks from to-day, the anniversaries will begin — public anniversaries and private. These, like perfumes, like music, will waken legions of visions. The days of the calendar, succeeding one another, will ring in the memories of hundreds and thousands like bells. Each date will invest its day and the sun or the rain thereof with special, pregnant relation to the bereft and the mourning of many faiths and languages. Thus all Europe will be tolling with memorial knells inaudible, yet which in those ears that hear them will sound louder than any noise of shrapnel or calamity.

II

II

CALAMITY, like those far-off locomotives on the Rhine, has again rolled out of Germany on her neighbors. Yet this very Calamity it is that has given me back my faith in my own country. It was Germany at peace which shook my faith; and I must tell you of that peaceful, beautiful Germany in which I rejoiced for so many days, and of how I envied it. Then, perhaps, among some other things I hope you will see, you will see that it is Germany who is, in truth, the deepest tragedy of this war.

The Germany at peace that I saw during May and June, 1914, was, in

the first place, a constant pleasure to
the eye, a constant repose to the body
and mind. Look where you might,
beauty was in some form to be seen,
given its chance by the intelligence of
man — not defaced, but made the most
of; and, whether in towns or in the
country, a harmonious spectacle was
the rule. I thought of our landscape,
littered with rubbish and careless fences
and stumps of trees, hideous with glar-
ing advertisements; of the rusty junk
lying about our farms and towns and
wayside stations; and of the disfigured
Palisades along the Hudson River.
America was ugly and shabby — made
so by Americans; Germany was swept
and garnished — made so by Germans.

In Nauheim the admirable courtyard
of the bathhouses was matched by the

admirable system within. The conven-
ience and the architecture were equally
good. For every hour of the invalid's
day the secret of his well-being seemed
to have been thought out. On one side
of the group and court of baths ran the
chief street, shady and well-kempt, with
its hotels and its very entertaining shops;
on the other side spread a park. This
was a truly gracious little region, em-
bowered in trees, with spaces and walks
and flowers all near at hand, yet nothing
crowded. The park sloped upward to
a terrace and casino, with tables for
sitting out to eat and drink and hear
the band, and with a concert hall and
theater for the evening. Herein come-
dies and little operas and music, both
serious and light, were played.

Nothing was far from anything; the

baths, the doctors, the hotels, the music, the tennis courts, the lake, the golf links — all were fitted into a scheme laid out with marvelous capability. Various hills and forests, a little more distant, provided walks for those robust enough to take them, while longer excursions in carriages or motor cars over miles of excellent roads were all mapped out and tariffed in a terse but comprehensive guidebook. Such was living at Nauheim. Dying, I feel sure, was equally well arranged; it was never allowed to obtrude itself on living.

Each day began with an early hour of routine, walking and water-drinking before breakfast, amid surroundings equally well planned — an arcade inclosing a large level space, with an expanse of water, a band playing, flowers growing in the open, cut flowers for sale in the arcade and comfortable seats where the doctor permitted pausing, but no permanent settling down. Thus went the whole day. Everything was well planned and everything worked. I thought of America, where so many things look beautiful on paper and so few things work, because nobody keeps the rules. I thought of our college elective system, by which every boy was free to study what best fitted him for his career, and nearly every boy did study what he could most easily pass examinations in. There was no elective system in Nauheim. Everybody kept the rules. There was no breakdown, no failure.

Moreover, the civility of the various ministrants to the invalid, from the eminent professor-doctor down through hotel porters and bath attendants to the elevator boy, was well-nigh perfect. If you asked for something out of the routine, either it was permitted or it was satisfactorily explained why it could not be permitted. Whether at the bank, the bookshop, the hotel, the railway station or in the street, your questions were not merely understood — the Germans knew the answers to them. And every day the street was charming with fresh flowers and fresh fruit in abundance at many corners and booths — cherries, strawberries, plums, apricots, grapes, both cheap and good, as here they never are. But the great luxury, the great repose, was that each person fitted his job, did it well, took it seriously. After our American way of taking it as a joke, particularly when you fumble it, this German way was almost enough to cure a sick man without further treatment.

III

III

THIS serenity of living was not got up for the stranger; it was not to meet his market that a complex and artificial ease had been constructed, bearing no relation to what lay beyond its limits. That sort of thing is to be found among ourselves in isolated spots, though far less perfect and far more expensive. Nauheim was merely a blossom on the general tree. It was when I began my walks in the country and found everywhere a corresponding, ordered excellence, and came to talk more and more with the peasants and to notice the men, women and children, that the scheme of Germany grew impressive to me.

So had it not been in 1870, as I looked back on my early impressions, reading them now in my maturer judgment's light. So had it not been even in 1882 and 1883, when I had again seen the country. We various invalids of Nauheim presently began to compare notes. All of us were going about the country, among the gardens and the farms, or across the plain through the fruit trees to little Friedberg on its hill — an old castle, a steep village, a clean Teutonic gem, dropped perfect out of the Middle Ages into the present, yet perfectly keeping up with the present. Many of the peasants in the plain, men and women, were of those who brought their flowers and produce to sell in Nauheim — humble people, poor in what you call worldly goods, but seemingly very few of them poor in the great essential possession.

We invalids compared notes and found ourselves all of one mind. Ten or twelve of us were, at the several hotels, acquaintances at home; every one had been struck with the contentment in the German face. Contentment! Among the old and young of both sexes this was the dominating note, the great essential possession. The question arose: What is the best sign that a government is doing well by its people — is agreeing with its people, so to speak? None of us were quite so sure as we used to be that our native formula, "Of the people, by the people, for the people," is the universal ultimate truth.

Twice two is four, wherever you go;

this is as certain in Berlin as it is at Washington or in the cannibal islands. But, until mankind grows uniform, can government be treated as you treat mathematics? Until mankind grows uniform, will any form of government be likely to fit the whole world like a glove? So long as mankind continues as various as men's digestions, better to look at government as if it were a sort of diet or treatment. How is the government agreeing with its people? This is the question to ask in each country. And what is the surest sign? Could any sign be surer than the general expression, the composite face of the people themselves? This goes deeper than skyscrapers and other material aspects.

I had sailed away from skyscrapers

and limited expresses; from farmers sowing crops wastefully; from houses burned through carelessness; from forests burned through carelessness; from heaps of fruit rotting on the ground in one place and hundreds of men hungry in another place. I had sailed away from the city face and the country face of America, and neither one was the face of content. They looked driven, unpeaceful, dissatisfied. The hasty American was not looking after his country himself, and nobody was there to make him look after it while he rushed about climbing, climbing — and to what? A higher skyscraper. It was very restful to come to a place where the spirit of man was in stable equilibrium; where man's lot was in stable equilibrium; where never a schoolboy had been told he might become President and every schoolboy knew he could not be Emperor.

The students on a walking holiday from their universities often wandered singing through Nauheim. Somewhat Tyrolese in get-up, sometimes with odd, Byronic collars, too much open at the neck, they wore their knapsacks and the caps that showed their guild. They came generally in the early morning while the invalids were strolling at the Sprudel. The sound of their young voices singing in part-chorus would be heard, growing near, passing close, then dying away melodiously among the trees.

A single little sharp discord vibrated through all this German harmony one day when I learned that in the Empire more children committed suicide than in any other country.

But soon this discord was lost amid the massive Teutonic polyphony of well-being. Of this well-being knowledge was enlarged by excursions to various towns. To Worms, for instance, that we might see the famous Luther Monument. Part of the journey thither lay through a fine forest. This the city of Frankfurt-am-Main owns and has forested for seven hundred years; using the wood all the time, but so wisely that the supply has maintained itself against the demand. I thought of our own forests, looted and leveled, and of ourselves boasting our glorious future while we obliterated that future's resources. Frankfurt was there to teach us better, had we chosen to learn.

c

IV

IV

IN Frankfurt-am-Main was born one of the three supreme poets since Greece and Rome — Goethe — from whom I shall quote more than once; but Frankfurt has present glories that I saw. It is one of many beautifully governed German cities. I grew even fond of its Union Station, since through this gate I entered so often the pleasures and edifications of the town. The trains were a symbol of the whole Empire. About a mile north of Nauheim the railroad passes under a bridge and curves out of sight. The four-fifteen was apt to be my express to Frankfurt. I would stand on the platform, watch in hand, looking northward for my train.

At four-eleven the bridge was invariably
an empty hole. Invariably at four-
twelve the engine filled the hole; then
the train glided in quietly, and smoothly
glided on, almost punctual to the second.
So did the other trains.

The conductors were officials of dis-
ciplined courtesy and informed minds.
They appeared at the door of your
compartment, erect, requesting your
ticket in an established formula. If
you asked them something they told
you correctly and with a Teutonic
adequacy that was grave, but not gruff.
Once only in a score of journeys did I
encounter bad manners. Now I should
never choose these admirable conductors for companions, but as conductors
they were superior to the engaging
fellow citizen who took my ticket down

in Georgia and, when I asked did his train usually make its scheduled connection at Yemassee Junction, cried out with contagious mirth:

"My Lawd, suh, 'most nevah!"

In these German trains another little discord jarred with some regularity: the German passengers they brought from Berlin, or were taking back to Berlin, were of a heavy impenetrable rudeness — quite another breed than the kindly Hessians of Frankfurt.

We know the saying of a floor — that it is so clean "you could eat your dinner off it." All the streets of Frankfurt, that I saw, were clean like this. The system of street cars was lucid — and blessedly noiseless! — and their conductors informed with the same adequate gravity I have already noted.

I found that I developed a special affection for Route 19, because this took me from the station to the opera house. But all routes took one to and through aspects of municipal perfection at which one stared with envy as one thought of home.

Oh, yes! Frankfurt is a name to me compact with memories — memories of clean streets; of streets full of by-passers who could direct you when you asked your way; of streets empty of beggars, empty of all signs of desolate, drunken or idle poverty; of streets bordered by substantial stone dwellings, with fragrant gardens; of excellent shops; the streets full of prosperous movement and bustle; an absence of rags, a presence of good stout clothes; a people of contented faces, whether they talked or were silent

— the same firm and broad contentment,
like a tree deep-rooted, in the city face
that was in the country face.

These burghers, these Frankfurters,
seemed to be going about their business
with a sort of solid yet placid energy,
well and deliberately aimed, that would
hit the mark at once without wasting
powder. It was very different and very
superior to the ill-arranged and hectic
haste of New York and Chicago; here
nobody seemed driven as though by
invisible furies — the German business
mind was not out of breath.

Such are my memories of Frankfurt
at work. Frankfurt at leisure was to be
seen in its Palm Garden. This was the
town's place of general recreation; large,
various, beautifully and intelligently
planned; with space for babies to roll

in safety, and there were the babies rolling, and their nurses; with courts for
tennis, and thither I saw adolescent
Frankfurt strolling in flannels and short
skirts after business hours; with benches
where sat the more elderly, taking the air
and gazing at the games or the flowers
or the pleasant trees; with paths more
sequestered that wound among bowers,
convenient for sweethearts — but I did
not see any, because I forbore to look. A
central building held tropic plants and
basins, and large rooms for bad weather,
I suppose, with a restaurant; but on
this fine day the music played and we
dined outside.

An entrance fee, very small, served to
make you respect the Palm Garden, since
humanity seldom respects what it pays
nothing for. Most unexpected show of

all in this Palm Garden were the flowers
under glass. I had erroneously supposed
that any German scheme of color would
be heavy, and possibly garish. Never
had I beheld more exquisite subtlety on
so extended a scale of arrangement.
One walked through aisle after aisle of
roses and other blooms in these green-
houses — everywhere was the same deli-
cate sense and feeling; the same, in fact,
in these flower schemes that one finds in
German lyric verse, and in the songs of
Schubert, Schumann and Franz.

It was in the opera house — Frankfurt
has a fine and commodious one — that
my whole impression of Germany's glory
culminated. The performances drew
their light from no Melbas or Carusos,
or other meteors, but from a fixed con-
stellation, now and then enriched by

some visitor; it was teamwork of drilled
and even excellence, singers, chorus,
orchestra and scenery unitedly equal to
the occasion, in operas old and new, an
immense sweep of repertory, with an
audience to match — an accustomed audience, to whom music was traditional
food, music having always grown here-
about plenteously, indigenously, so that
they took it as naturally as they took
their Rhine wine, paying for it as moder-
ately, going to hear it in rather plain
clothes, as a rule — men in day dress,
women in high-neck; not an audience
that had to put on its diamonds in order
to listen conspicuously to a costly and
not comprehended exotic.

The difference between hearing opera
where it grows and hearing it in New
York is the difference between eating

strawberries warm from their vines in June and strawberries in January that have come a thousand miles by freight. Where opera grows, it is the blend of native music, singers and listeners that gives a ripe flavor of a warmth which Fifth Avenue can never purchase.

This, every performance in Frankfurt had; but even this could be raised to a higher key of inspiration. I walked in one night and found myself amid a pious ceremonial. They were giving an old work, of bygone design, stiff in outline, noble, remote from all present things. Why did they revive this somewhat pale and rigid classic? For contrast, variety? Not at all. Two hundred years ago this day, Gluck had been born. Gluck had written this opera. For this reason, then, Frankfurt was assembled to hear

Gluck's music and remember him; and, as I looked at these living Germans honoring their classics, I thought it was truly a splendid people that not only possessed but practically nourished themselves with these masterpieces of their great dead.

But this was not all. This was Germany looking at its Past. In the Frankfurt opera house I also learned one of the ways in which Germany attends to its Future. It was on a Sunday afternoon. As I crossed the open space toward the opera house it seemed as though I were the only grown person bound there. Children by threes and fours, and in little groups, were streaming from every quarter, entering every door, tripping up the wide, handsome stairs, filling all the seats — boys and girls; it was like the Pied Piper of Hamelin. After a few minutes

I found that I was indeed almost alone amid a rippling sea of children — nearly two thousand, as I later learned. In the boxes here and there was a parent or two with a family party, and dotted about the house a few scattered older heads among the young ones.

The overture began. "Hush!" went several little voices; the sprightly, expectant Babel fell to silence; they listened like a congregation in church.

Then the curtain rose. It was a gay old opera, tuneful, full of boisterous, innocent comedy and simple sentiment. Not Gluck this time; Gluck would have been a trifle severe for their young understandings. The enthusiasm and the attention of these boys and girls, with their clapping of hands and their laughter, soon affected the spirits of the singers

as a radiant day in spring; it affected me.
I envied the happy parents who had their
children round them; it was like some
sort of wonderful April light. Beneath
it the quaint, sweet old opera shone like
a fruit tree in blossom. The actors
became as children again themselves; so
did the fiddlers; so did the conductor.
I doubt if that little old opera, *Czaar und
Zimmermann,* had ever felt younger in
its life; and I thought if the spirit of
Goethe were watching Frankfurt, his
city, to-day, it would add a new happiness to a moment of his Eternity.

Between the acts I was full of questions. What occasion was this? I read
the program, wherein was set forth a most
interesting account of the composer —
his character, life and adventures, with a
historic account also of Peter the Great,

the hero of the opera; but nothing about
the occasion. So in the lobby I ad-
dressed myself to a group of the men
I had seen dotted among the rows of
children. The men were schoolmasters.
The occasion was an experiment. The
children were of the public schools of
Frankfurt — not the oldest scholars, but
the middle grades of the schools. For
the oldest, Frankfurt had already provided opera days, but this was the first
ever given for these younger boys and
girls. The cost was twelve-and-a-half
cents a seat. If it proved a success, a
second would follow in two weeks. At
the theater, throughout each winter
school term, plays were given expressly
for them in this way — the great German
classics; but never any opera before
to-day.

D

Well, the performance went on; but I was obliged, near the end of it, to hasten away to my train for Nauheim, most reluctantly leaving the sight and company of those two thousand joyous children of the Frankfurt public schools. "Rosy cheeks predominated; eyeglasses were rare." — Again I quote from my own diary: — "The children seemed between ten and fifteen. The boys had good foreheads and big backs to their heads."

v

V

NOTHING can efface this memory, nothing can efface the whole impression of Germany; in retrospect this picture rises clear — the fair aspect and order of the country and the cities, the well-being of the people, their contented faces, their grave adequacy, their kindliness; and, crowning all material prosperity, the feeling for beauty as shown by their gardens, and, better and more important still, the reverent value for their great native poets and musicians, so attentive, so cherishing, seeing to it that the young generation began early its acquaintance with the masterpieces that are Germany's heritage of inspiration.

Such was the splendor of this empire as it unrolled before me through May and June, 1914, that by contrast the state of its two great neighbors, France and England, seemed distressing and unenviable. Paris was shabby and incoherent, London full of unrest. Instead of Germany's order, confusion prevailed in France; instead of Germany's placidity, disturbance prevailed in England; and in both France and England incompetence seemed the chief note. The French face, alike in city or country, was too often a face of worried sadness or revolt; men spoke of political scandals and dissensions petty and unpatriotic in spirit, and a political trial, revealing depths of every sort of baseness and dishonor, filled the newspapers; while in England, besides discord of suffrage and discord of labor, civil war seemed so imminent that no one would have been surprised to hear of it any day.

So that I thought: Suppose a soul, arrived on earth from another world, wholly ignorant of earth, without any mortal ties whatever, were given its choice after a survey of the nations, which it should be born in and belong to? In May, June and July, 1914, my choice would have been, not France, not England, not America, but Germany.

It was on the seventh day of June, 1914, that Frankfurt assembled her school children in the opera house, to further their taste and understanding of Germany's supreme national art. Exactly eleven months later, on May 7, 1915, a German torpedo sank the Lusitania; and the cities of the Rhine celebrated this also for their school children.

VI

VI

T HE world is in agony. We witness the most terrible catastrophe known to mankind — most terrible, not from its huge size, but because it is a moral catastrophe. Through centuries of suffering and cruelty, guided by religion, we thought we had attained to knowledge of and belief in a public right between nations, and an honorable warfare, if warfare must be. This has been shattered to pieces. No need to investigate further the atrocities at Liège or Louvain. These and more have indeed been amply proved, but what need of proof after the Lusitania school festival? In that holiday we see the feast of *Kultur*, the Teutonic climax. How came it to pass? Is it the same Germany who gave those two holidays to her school children? The opera in Frankfurt, and this orgy of barbaric blood-lust, guttural with the deep basses of the fathers and shrill with the trebles of their young? Their young, to whom they teach one day the gentle melodies of Lortzing, and to exult in world-assassination on another?

Goethe said — and the words glow with new prophetic light: "Germans are of yesterday; . . . a few centuries must still elapse before . . . it will be said of them, 'It is long since they were barbarians.'" And again: "National hatred is a peculiar thing. You will always find it strongest and most violent where there is the lowest degree of *Kul-*

tur." But how came it to pass? Do the two holidays proceed from the same *Kultur,* the same Fatherland?

They do; and nothing in the whole story of mankind is more strange than the case of Germany — how Germany through generations has been carefully trained for this wild spring at the throat of Europe that she has made. The Servian assassination has nothing to do with it, save that it accidentally struck the hour. Months and years before that, Germany was crouching for her spring. In one respect the war she has incubated is the old assault of Xerxes, of Alexander, of Napoleon, of every one who has been visited by the dangerous dream of world conquest. Only, never before has the dream been taught to a people on such a scale, not merely because of the vast modern apparatus, but much more because no subjects of any despot have ever been so politically docile and credulous as the Germans.

In another respect this war resembles strikingly our own and the French Revolution. All three were prepared and fomented by books, by teachings from books. The American brain seized hold of certain doctrines and generalizations of Locke, Montesquieu, Burlamaqui and Beccaria concerning the rights of man and the consent of the governed. The French brain nourished and inspired itself with some theorems of the encyclopedists and of Rousseau about man's natural innocence and the social contract. The Teutonic brain assimilated some diplomatic and philosophic precepts laid down by Machiavelli,

Nietzsche and Treitschke. Indeed, Fichte, during the Winter of 1807–08, at the University of Berlin, made an address to the German people which may be accounted the first famous academic harbinger and source of the present Teutonic state of mind. Here the parallel stops. With America and France, war made way for independence, liberty and freedom, political and moral; Germany would establish everywhere her absolute military despotism. We shall reach in due course the full statement of her creed; we are not ready for it yet.

VII

VII

OFTEN of late I have thought of those twenty-one locomotives moving along the bank of the Rhine. They were a symbol. They stood for the House of Hohenzollern; they carried Cæsar and all his fortunes, which had begun long before locomotives were invented. July 19, 1870, is one of the dates that does not remain of the same size, but grows, has not done growing yet, will be one of History's enormous dates before it is done growing. The heavier descendants of those locomotives have been lugging to France a larger destruction, and more hideous, than their ancestors dragged there; but this new freight belongs to the same haul, forms part of one vast organic materialistic growth, and spiritual eclipse, of which 1870 and 1914 are important parts, but by no means the whole.

Woven with it is the struggle of nations for the possession of their own soul. Consider 1870 in this light: Through that war France took her soul out of the custody of an Emperor and handed it to the people; through the same war Germany placed her soul in the hands of an Emperor. Defeated France, rid of her Bonapartes; victorious Germany, shackled to her Hohenzollern! In the light of forty-five years how those two opposite actions gleam with significance, and how in the same light the two words *defeat* and *victory* grow lambent with shifting import! Unless our democratic faith be vain, France walked forward then, and Germany backward. But this did not seem so last June.

VIII

VIII

HAD it not culminated before our eyes, the case of Germany would be perfectly incredible. As it stands to-day, the truly incredible thing is that she should have made her spring at the throat of an unexpecting, unprepared world. Now that she *has* sprung, the diagnosis of her case has been often and ably made — before the event, Dr. Charles Sarolea, a Belgian gentleman, made it notably; but prophets are seldom recognized except by posterity. The case of Germany is a hospital case, a case for the alienist; the mania of grandeur, complemented by the mania of persecution.

Very well do I remember the first dawning hint I had of this diseased mental state. It was Wednesday, August 5, 1914. We were in mid-ocean. Before the bulletin board we passengers were clustered to read that day's marconigram and learn what more of Europe had fallen to pieces since yesterday. This morning was posted the Kaiser's proclamation, quoting Hamlet, calling on his subjects "to be or not to be," and to defy a world conspired against them. In these words there was such a wild, incoherent ring of exaltation that I said to a friend: "Can he be off his head?"

Later in that voyage we sped silent and unlanterned through the fog from two German cruisers, of which nobody seemed personally afraid but one stewardess. She said: "They're all wild beasts. They would send us all to the bottom." No one believed her. Since then we believe her. Since then we have heard the wild incoherent ring in many German voices besides the Kaiser's, and we know to-day that Germany's mania is analogous to those mental epidemics of the Middle Ages, when fanaticism, usually religious, sent entire communities into various forms of madness.

The case of Germany is the Prussianizing of Germany. Long after all of us are gone, men will still be studying this war; and, whatever responsibility for it be apportioned among the nations, the huge weight and bulk of guilt will be laid on Prussia and the Hohenzollern — unless, indeed, it befall that Germany conquer the world and the Kaiser dictate his version of History to us all,

suppressing all other versions, as he
has conducted the training of his subjects since 1888. But this will not be;
whatever comes first, this cannot be
the end. If I believed that the earth
would be Prussianized, life would cease
to be desirable.

To me the whole case of Germany,
the whole process, seems a fatalistic
thing, destined, inevitable; cosmic forces
above and beyond men's comprehension
flooding this northern land with their
high tide, as once they flooded southern
coasts; giving to this Teuton race its
turn, its day, its hour of white heat
and of bloom, its temperamental greatness, its strength and excess of vital
sap, intellectual, procreative — all this
grandeur to be hurled into tragedy by
its own action.

The process goes back a long way behind Napoleon — who stayed it for a while — to years when we see the Germany of the Reformation, Poetry, Music, the grand Germany, blossoming in the very same moment that the Prussian poison was also germinating. About 1830, Heine perceived and wrote scornfully concerning the new and evil influence. This was a germination of state and family ambition combined, fermenting at last into lust for world dominion. It grows quite visible first in Frederick the Great. By him the Prussian state of mind and international ethics began to be formulated. By force and fraud he annexed weak peoples' territory. He cut Poland's body in three, blasphemously inviting Russia and Austria to partake with him of his Eucharist.

Theft has followed theft since Frederick's. His cynical, strong spirit guided Prussia after Waterloo, guided first the predecessor of Bismarck and next Bismarck himself, with his stealing of Schleswig-Holstein, his dishonest mutilation of the telegram at Ems and the subsequent rape of Alsace and Lorraine in 1870. Very plain it is to see now, and very sad, why the small separate German states that had indeed produced their giants — their Luthers, Goethes, Beethovens — but had always suffered military defeat, had been the shambles of their conquerors for centuries, should after 1870 hail their new-created Emperor. Had he not led them united to the first glory and conquest they had ever known? Had he not got them back Alsace and Lorraine, which

France had stolen from them two hundred years ago? So they handed their soul to the Hohenzollern. This marks the beginning of the end.

IX

IX

WE can hardly emphasize too much, or sufficiently underline, the moral effect of 1870 on the German nature, the influence it had on the German mind. It is essential to a clear understanding of the full Prussianizing process that now set in. On the German's innate docility and credulity many have dwelt, but few on what 1870 did to this. Only with Bismarck's quick, tremendous victory over France as the final explanation is the abject and servile faith that the Germans thenceforth put in Prussia rendered conceivable to reason. They blindly swallowed the sham that Bismarck gave them as universal suffrage.

They swallowed extreme political and military restraint. They swallowed a rigid compulsion in schools, which led to the excess in child suicide I have mentioned. They swallowed a state of life where outside the indicated limits almost nothing was permitted and almost everything was forbidden.

But all this proscription is merely material and has been attended by great material welfare. Intellectual speculation was apparently unfettered; but he who dared philosophize about Liberty and the Divine right of Kings found it was not. Prussia put its uniform not only on German bodies but on their brains. Literature and music grew correspondingly sterilized. Drama, fiction, poetry and the comic papers became invaded by a new violence and a new, heavy obscenity. Impatience with the noble German classics was bred by Prussia. What wonder, since freedom was their essence?

Beethoven, after Napoleon made himself Emperor, tore off the dedication of his "Eroica" symphony to Napoleon. And Goethe had said: "Napoleon affords us an example of the danger of elevating oneself to the Absolute and sacrificing everything to the carrying out of an idea." Goethe fell frankly out of date in Berlin. Symphony orchestras could no longer properly interpret Mozart and Beethoven. A strange blend of frivolity and bestiality began to pervade the whole realm of German art. Scientific eminence degenerated *pari passu*. No originator of the dimensions of Helmholtz was produced, but a herd of diligent and thorough workers-out of the ideas got from England — like the aniline dyes — or from France — like the Wassermann tests — and seldom credited to their sources. So poor grew the academic tone at Berlin that a Munich professor declined an offer of promotion thither.

For forty years German school children and university students sat in the thickening fumes that exhaled from Berlin, spread everywhere by professors chosen at the fountainhead. Any professor or editor who dared speak anything not dictated by Prussia, for German credulity to write down on its slate, was dealt with as a heretic.

Out of the fumes emerged three colossal shapes — the Super-man, the Super-race and the Super-state: the new Trinity of German worship.

X

X

THUS was Germany shut in from the world. Even her Socialist-Democrats abjectly conformed. China built a stone wall, Germany a wall of the mind.

To assert that any great nation has in these modern days deliberately built around herself such a wall, may seem an extreme statement, and I will therefore support it with an instance — only one instance out of many, out of hundreds; it will suffice to indicate the sort of information about the world lying outside the wall that Germany has carefully prepared for the children in her schools. I quote from the letter of an American parent recently living in Berlin, who placed his children in a school there: "The text books were unique. I suppose there was not in any book of physics or chemistry that they studied an admission that a citizen of some other country had taken any forward step; every step was by some line of argument assigned to a German. As you might expect, the history of the modern world is the work of German Heroes. The oddest example, however, was the geography used by Katherine. (His daughter, aged thirteen.) This contained maps indicating the Deutsche Gebiete (the German "spheres of influence" in foreign lands) in striking colors. In North and South America, including the United States and Canada, there are said to be three classes of inhabitants — negroes, Indians and Germans. For the United States there is a black belt for negroes and a middle-west section for Indians; but the rest is Deutsche Gebiete. Canada is occupied mainly by Indians. The matter was brought to my attention because one of Katherine's girl friends asked her whether she was of negro or Indian blood; and when she replied she was neither her friend pointed out that this was impossible for she surely was not German." Information less laughable about the morals taught in the German schools I forbear to quote.

During forty years Germany sat within her wall, learning and repeating Prussian incantations. It recalls those savage rites where the participants, by shouting and by concerted rhythmic movements, work themselves into a frothing state. This has befallen Germany. Within her wall of moral isolation her sight has grown distorted, her sense of proportion is lost; a set of reeling delusions possesses her — her own greatness, her mission of *Kultur*, her contempt for the rest of mankind, her grievance that mankind is in league to cramp and suppress her.

These delusions have been attended by their proper Nemesis: Germany has misunderstood us all — everybody and everything outside her wall.

Like the bewitched dwarfs in certain old magic tales, whose talk reveals their evil without their knowing it, Germans constantly utter words of the most naïf and grotesque self-betrayal — as when the German ambassador was being es-

corted away from England and was
urged by his escort not to be so down-
cast; the war being no fault of his.
He answered in sincere sadness:

"Oh, you don't realize! My future
is broken. I was sent to watch England
and tell my Emperor the right moment
for him to strike, when England's in-
ternal disturbances would make it impossible for her to fight us. I told him
the moment had come."

Or again, when a German in Brussels
said to an American:

· "We were sincerely sorry for Belgium;
but we feel it is better for that country
to suffer, even to disappear, than for
our Empire, so much larger and more
important, to be torpedoed by our
treacherous enemies."

Or again, when Doctor Dernburg

shows us why Germany had to murder eleven hundred passengers:

"It has been the custom heretofore to take off passengers and crew. . . . But a submarine . . . cannot do it. The submarine is a frail craft and may easily be rammed, and a speedy ship is capable of running away from it."

No more than the dwarf has Germany any conception what such candid words reveal of herself to ears outside her Teutonic wall — that she has walked back to the morality of the Stone Age and made ancient warfare more hideous through the devices of modern science.

Thus her Nemesis is to misunderstand the world. She blundered as to what Belgium would do, what France would do, what Russia would do; and she most desperately blundered as to what

England would do. And she expected American sympathy.

Summarized thus, the Prussianizing of Germany seems fantastic; fantastic, too, and not of the real world, the utter credulity, the abject, fervent faith of the hypnotized young men. Yet here are a young German's recent words. I have seen his letter, written to a friend of mine. He was tutor to my friend's children. Delightful, of admirable education, there was no sign in him of hypnotism. He went home to fight. There he inhaled afresh the Prussian fumes. Presently his letter came, just such a letter as one would wish from an ardent, sincere, patriotic youth — for the first pages. Then the fumes show their work and he suddenly breaks out in the following intellectual vertigo:

"Individual life has become worthless; even the uneducated men feel that something greater than individual happiness is at stake, and the educated know that it is the culture of Europe. By her shameless lies and cold-blooded hypocrisy England has forfeited her claim to the title of a country of culture. France has passed her prime anyway, your country is too far behind in its development, the other countries are too small to carry on the heritage of Greek culture and Christian faith — the two main components of every higher culture to-day; so *we* have to do it, and we *shall* do it — even if we and millions more of us should have to die."

There you have it! A cultivated student, a noble nature, a character of promise, Prussianized, with millions like him, into a gibbering maniac, and flung into a caldron of blood! Could tragedy be deeper? Goethe's young Wilhelm Meister thus images the ruin of Hamlet's mind and how it came about: "An oak tree is planted in a costly vase, which should only have borne beautiful flowers in its bosom; the roots expand and the vase is shattered." Thus has Prussia, planted in Germany, cracked the Empire.

G

XI

ND now we are ready for the Prussian Creed. The following is an embodiment, a composite statement, of Prussianism, compiled sentence by sentence from the utterances of Prussians, the Kaiser and his generals, professors, editors, and Nietzsche, part of it said in cold blood, years before this war, and all of it a declaration of faith now being ratified by action:

"We Hohenzollerns take our crown from God alone. On me the Spirit of God has descended. I regard my whole . . . task as appointed by heaven. Who opposes me I shall crush to pieces.

Nothing must be settled in this world without the intervention . . . of . . . the German Emperor. He who listens to public opinion runs a danger of inflicting immense harm on . . . the State. When one occupies certain positions in the world one ought to make dupes rather than friends. Christian morality cannot be political. Treaties are only a disguise to conceal other political aims. Remember that the German people are the chosen of God.

"Might is right and . . . is decided by war. Every youth who enters a beer-drinking and dueling club will receive the true direction of his life. War in itself is a good thing. God will see to it that war always recurs. The efforts directed toward the abolition of war must not only be termed foolish, but absolutely immoral. The peace of Europe is only a secondary matter for us. The sight of suffering does one good; the infliction of suffering does one more good. This war must be conducted as ruthlessly as possible.

"The Belgians should not be shot *dead*. They should be . . . so left as to make impossible all hope of recovery. The troops are to treat the Belgian civil population with unrelenting severity and frightfulness. Weak nations have not the same right to live as powerful . . . nations. The world has no longer need of little nationalities. We Germans have little esteem and less respect . . . for Holland. We need to enlarge our colonial possessions; such territorial acquisitions we can only realize at the cost of other states.

"Russia must no longer be our frontier. The Polish press should be annihilated . . . likewise the French and Danish. . . . The Poles should be allowed . . . three privileges: to pay taxes, serve in the army, and shut their jaws. France must be so completely crushed that she will never again cross our path. You must remember that we have not come to make war on the French people, but to bring them the higher Civilization. The French have shown themselves decadent and without respect for the Divine law. Against England we fight for booty. Our real enemy is England. We have to . . . crush absolutely perfidious Albion . . . subdue her to such an extent that her influence all over the world is broken forever.

"German should replace English as

the world language. English, the bastard tongue . . . must be swept into the remotest corners . . . until it has returned to its original elements of an insignificant pirate dialect. The German language acts as a blessing which, coming direct from the hand of God, sinks into the heart like a precious balm. To us, more than any other nation, is intrusted the true structure of human existence. Our own country, by employing military power, has attained a degree of Culture which it could never have reached by peaceful means.

"The civilization of mankind suffers every time a German becomes an American. Let us drop our miserable attempts to excuse Germany's action. We willed it. Our might shall create

a new law in Europe. It is Germany
that strikes. We are morally and in-
tellectually superior beyond all com-
parison. . . . We must . . . fight with
Russian beasts, English mercenaries and
Belgian fanatics. We have nothing to
apologize for. It is no consequence
whatever if all the monuments ever
created, all the pictures ever painted,
all the buildings ever erected by the
great architects of the world, be destroyed. . . . The ugliest stone placed
to mark the burial of a German grenadier
is a more glorious monument than all
the cathedrals of Europe put together.
No respect for the tombs of Shake-
speare, Newton and Faraday.

"They call us barbarians. What of
it? The German claim must be: . . .
Education to hate. . . . Organization

of hatred. . . . Education to the desire for hatred. Let us abolish unripe and false shame. . . . To us is given faith, hope and hatred; but hatred is the greatest among them."

XII

XII

CAN the splendid land of Goethe unlearn its Prussian lesson and regain its own noble sanity, or has it too long inhaled the fumes? There is no saying yet. Still they sit inside their wall. Like a trained chorus they still repeat that England made the war, that Louvain was not destroyed, that Rheims was not bombarded, that their Fatherland is the unoffending victim of world-jealousy. When travelers ask what proofs they have, the trained chorus has but one reply: "Our government officials tell us so." Berlin, Cologne, Munich — all their cities — give this answer to the traveler. Nothing that we know do they know. It is kept from them. Their brains still wear the Prussian uniform and go mechanically through the Prussian drill. Will adversity lift this curse?

Something happened at Louvain — a little thing, but let it give us hope. In the house of a professor at the University some German soldiers were quartered, friendly, considerate, doing no harm. Suddenly one day, in obedience to new orders, they fell on this home, burned books, wrecked rooms, destroyed the house and all its possessions. Its master is dead. His wife, looking on with her helpless children, saw a soldier give an apple to a child.

"Thank you," she said; "you, at least, have a heart."

"No, madam," said the German; "it is broken."

Goethe said: "He who wishes to exert a useful influence must be careful to insult nothing. . . . We are become too humane to enjoy the triumphs of Cæsar." Ninety years after he said this Germany took the Belgian women from their ruined villages — some of these women being so infirm that for months they had not been out-of-doors — and loaded them on trains like cattle, and during several weeks exposed them publicly to the jeers and scoffs and insults of German crowds through city after city.

Perhaps the German soldier whose heart was broken by Louvain will be one of a legion, and thus, perhaps, through thousands of broken German

H

hearts, Germany may become herself again. She has hurled calamity on a continent. She has struck to pieces a Europe whose very unpreparedness answers her ridiculous falsehood that she was attacked first. Never shall Europe be again as it was. Our brains, could they take in the whole of this war, would burst.

But Calamity has its Pentecost. When its mighty wind rushed over Belgium and France, and its tongues of fire sat on each of them, they, too, like the apostles in the New Testament, began to speak as the Spirit gave them utterance. Their words and deeds have filled the world with a splendor the world had lost. The flesh, that has dominated our day and generation, fell away in the presence of the Spirit. I have heard Belgians bless the martyrdom and awakening of their nation. They have said:

"Do not talk of our suffering; talk of our glory. We have found ourselves."

Frenchmen have said to me: "For forty-four years we have been unhappy, in darkness, without health, without faith, believing the true France dead. Resurrection has come to us." I heard the French Ambassador, Jules Jusserand, say in a noble speech: "George Eliot profoundly observes that to every man comes a crisis when in a moment, without chance for reflection, he must decide and act instantly. What determines his decision? His whole past, the daily choices between good and evil that he has made throughout his previous years — these determine his decision. Such a crisis fell in a moment on France; she acted instantly, true to her historic honor and courage."

Every day deeds of faith, love and renunciation are done by the score and the hundred which will never be recorded, and every one of which is noble enough to make an immortal song. All over the broken map of Europe, through stricken thousands of square miles, such deeds are being done by Servians, Russians, Poles, Belgians, French and English, — yes, and Germans too, — the souls of men and women rising above their bodies, flinging them away for the sake of a cause. Think of one incident only, only one of the white-hot gleams of the Spirit that have reached us from the raging furnace. Out from the burning

cathedral of Rheims they were dragging
the wounded German prisoners lying
helpless inside on straw that had begun
to burn. In front of the church the
French mob was about to shoot or tear
to pieces those crippled, defenseless
enemies. You and I might well want
to kill an enemy who had set fire to
Mount Vernon, the house of the Father
of our Country.

For more than seven hundred years
that great church of Rheims had been
the sacred shrine of France. One minute
more and those Germans lying or crawl-
ing outside the church door would have
been destroyed by the furious people.
But above the crash of rafters and glass,
the fall of statues, the thunder of bom-
barding cannon, and the cries of French
execration, rose one man's voice. There

on the steps of the ruined church stood a priest. He lifted his arms and said:

"Stop; remember the ancient ways and chivalry of France. It is not Frenchmen who trample on a maimed and fallen foe. Let us not descend to the level of our enemies."

It was enough. The French remembered France. Those Germans were conveyed in safety to their appointed shelter — and far away, across the lands and oceans, hearts throbbed and eyes grew wet that had never looked on Rheims.

These are the tongues of fire; this is the Pentecost of Calamity. Often it must have made brothers again of those who found themselves prone on the battlefield, neighbors awaiting the grave. In Flanders a French officer of cavalry, shot through the chest, lay dying, but with life enough still to write his story to the lady of his heart. He wrote thus:

"There are two other men lying near me, and I do not think there is much hope for them either. One is an officer of a Scottish regiment and the other a private in the uhlans. They were struck down after me, and when I came to myself I found them bending over me, rendering first aid. The Britisher was pouring water down my throat from his flask, while the German was endeavoring to stanch my wound with an antiseptic preparation served out to their troops by the medical corps. The Highlander had one of his legs shattered, and the German had several pieces of shrapnel buried in his side.

"In spite of their own sufferings, they were trying to help me; and when I was fully conscious again the German gave us a morphia injection and took one himself. His medical corps had also provided him with the injection and the needle, together with printed instructions for their use. After the injection, feeling wonderfully at ease, we spoke of the lives we had lived before the war. We all spoke English, and we talked of the women we had left at home. Both the German and the Britisher had been married only a year. . . .

"I wondered — and I suppose the others did — why we had fought each other at all. I looked at the High-lander, who was falling to sleep, exhausted, and, in spite of his drawn face and mud-stained uniform, he looked the embodiment of freedom. Then I thought of the Tricolor of France and all that France had done for liberty. Then I watched the German, who had ceased to speak. He had taken a prayer book from his knapsack, and was trying to read a service for soldiers wounded in battle. And . . . while I watched him I realized what we were fighting for. . . . He was dying in vain, while the Britisher and myself, by our deaths, would probably contribute something toward the cause of civilization and peace."

Thus wrote this young French officer of cavalry to the lady of his heart, the American lady to whom he was engaged. The Red Cross found the letter at his side. Through it she learned the manner of his death. This, too, is the Pentecost of Calamity.

XIII

XIII

AND what do the women say — the women who lose such men? Thus do they decline to attend at The Hague the Peace Congress of foolish women who have lost nobody:

"How would it be possible, in an hour like this, for us to meet women of the enemy's countries? . . . Have they disavowed the . . . crimes of their government? Have they protested against the violation of Belgium's neutrality? Against offenses to the law of nations? Against the crimes of their army and navy? If their voices had been raised it was too feebly for the echo of their protest to reach us across our violated and devastated territories. . . ."

And one celebrated lady writes to a delegate at The Hague:

"Madam, are you really English? . . . I confess I understand better English-women who wish to fight. . . . To ask Frenchwomen in such an hour to come and talk of arbitration and mediation and discourse of an armistice is to ask them to deny their nation. . . . All that Frenchwomen could desire is to awake and acclaim in their children, their husbands and brothers, and in their very fathers, the conviction that defensive war is a thing so holy that all must be abandoned, forgotten, sacrificed, and death must be faced heroically to defend and save that which is most sacred . . . our country. . . . It would

be to deny my dead to look for anything beside that which is and ought
to be!—if the God of right and justice, the enemy of the devil and of
force and crazy pride, is the true God."

Thus awakened and transfigured by
Calamity do men and women rise in
their full spiritual nature, efface themselves, and utter sacred words. Calamity, when the Lusitania went down,
wrung from the lips of an awakened
German, Kuno Francke, this noble burst
of patriotism:

*Ends Europe so? Then, in Thy mercy,
    God,
Out of the foundering planet's gruesome
    night
Pluck Thou my people's soul. From rage
    and craze*

Of the staled Earth, O lift Thou it aloft,
Re-youthed, and through transfiguration
    cleansed;
So beaming shall it light the newer time,
And heavenly, on a world refreshed, un-
    fold.
Soul of my race, thou sinkest not to dust.

If Germany's tragedy be, as I think, the deepest of all, the hope is that she, too, will be touched by the Pentecost of Calamity, and pluck her soul from Prussia, to whom she gave it in 1870. Thus shall the curse be lifted.

XIV

ND what of ourselves in this well-nigh world-wide cloud-burst?

Every man has walked at night through gloom where objects were dim and hard to see, when suddenly a flash of lightning has struck the landscape livid. Trees close by, fences far off, houses, fields, animals and the faces of people — all things stand transfixed by a piercing distinctness. So now, in this thunderstorm of war, each nation and every man and woman is searchingly revealed by the perpetual lightnings. Whatever this American nation is, whatever aspect, noble or ignoble, our Democracy shows in the glare of this cataclysm, is even already engraved on the page of History, will be the portrait of the United States in 1914–15 for all time.

I want no better photograph of any individual than his opinion of this war. If he has none, that is a photograph of him. Last autumn there were Americans who wished the papers would stop printing war news and give their readers a change. So we have their photographs, as well as those of other Americans who merely calculated the extra dollars they could squeeze out of Europe's need and agony. But that — thank God ! — is not what we look like as a whole. Our sympathy has poured out for Belgium a springtide of help and relief; it has flowed to the wounded and afflicted

of Poland, Servia, France and England.
A continuous publishing of books, maga-
zine articles and editorials, full of justice and of anger at Prussia's long-
prepared and malignant assault, should
prove to Europe that American hearts
and heads by the thousand and hundred
thousand are in the right place. Merely
the stand taken by the *New York Sun*,
New York Times, Outlook and *Philadel-
phia Public Ledger* — to name no more
— saves us from the reproach of moral
neutrality: saves us as individuals.

Yet, somehow, in Europe's eyes we
fall short. The Allies, in spite of their
recognition of our material generosity,
find us spiritually wanting. In the
London Punch, on the sinking of the
Lusitania, Britannia stands perplexed
and indignant behind the bowed figure

of America, and, with a hand on her
shoulder, addresses her thus:

In silence you have looked on felon blows,
  On butcher's work of which the waste
    lands reek;
Now, in God's name, from Whom your
    greatness flows,
  Sister, will you not speak?

This is asked of us not as individuals
but as a nation; and as a nation our
only spokesman is our Government:
"Sister, will you not speak?" Well —
we did speak; but after nine months
of silence. This silence, in the opinion
of French and Belgian emissaries who
have talked to me with courteous frank-
ness, constitutes our moral failure.

"When this war began" — they say
— "we all looked to you. You were the

great Democracy; you were not involved; you would speak the justifying word we longed for. We knew you must keep out politically; this was your true part and your great strength. We altogether agreed with your President there. But why did your universities remain dumb? The University of Chicago stopped the mouth of a Belgian professor who was going to present Belgium's case in public. Your press has been divided. The word we expected from you has never come. You sent us your charity; but what we wanted was justice, ratification of our cause."

To this I have answered:

"First — Our universities do not and cannot sit like yours in high seats, inspiring public opinion. I wish they did. Second — We are not yet melted into one nationality; we are a mosaic of languages and bloods; yet, even so, never in my life have I seen the American press and people so united on any question. Third — Our charity is our very way — the only way we have — of telling you we are with you. I am glad you recognize the necessity of our political neutrality. Anything else would have been, both historically and as an act of folly, unprecedented. Fourth — Do not forget that George Washington advised us to mind our own business."

But they reply: "Isn't this your own business?" And there they touch the core of the matter.

Across the sea the deadliest assault ever made on Democracy has been going on, month after month. We send bread and bandages to the

wounded; individually we denounce the
assault. Columbia and Uncle Sam stand
looking on. Is this quite enough? War
being out of the question, was there
nothing else? No protest to register?
Did the wide ocean wholly let Columbia
out? Europe, weltering in her own
failure, had turned towards us a wistful
look.

I cannot tell what George Washington
would have thought; I only know that
my answer to my European friends
leaves them unconvinced — and therefore how can it quite satisfy me? Minds
are exalted now, and white-hot. When
they cool, what will our historic likeness
be as revealed in the lightnings of this
cosmic emergency? Will it be the portrait of a people who sold its birthright
for a mess of pottage? Viewing how

we have given, and the tone of our press, perhaps this would hardly be just. Yet I can not but regret that we did not protest. What we lost in not doing so I see clearly; I can not see clearly what we gained. We may argue thus in our defense: If it is deemed that we missed a great opportunity in not protesting as signatories of the violated Hague conventions, are not our proofs of the violations more authentic now than at the time? What we heard was incredible to American minds. We had never made or known such war. By the time the truth was established a protest might have seemed somewhat belated. Well, this is all the explanation we can offer. Is it enough?

It is too early to answer; certain it is that not as we see ourselves but as

others see us, so shall we forever be.
Certain it is also, and eternally, that
through suffering alone men and nations
find their greater selves. It is fifty years
since we Americans knew the Pentecost
of Calamity. These years have been too
easy. We have not had to live danger-
ously enough. We have prospered, we
have been immune, and our prosperity
has proved somewhat a curse in disguise.

In these times that uncover men's
souls and the souls of nations, has our
soul come to light, or only our huge,
lavish body? In 1865 we had found
our soul indeed. Where is it gone? We
have been witnessing many "scholarly
retreats," and every day we have had
to hear the "maxims of a low prudence."
Have they sunk to the core and killed
it? God forbid! But since August, 1914,

we have stood listening to the cry of our European brothers-in-Liberty. They did not ask our feeble arm to strike in their cause, but they yearned for our voice and did not get it. Will History acquit us of this silence?

Meanwhile, the maxims of a low prudence, masquerading as Christianity, daily counsel us to keep our arm feeble. It was not so that Washington survived Valley Forge, or Lincoln won through to Appomattox. If the Fourth of July and the Declaration it celebrates still mean anything to us, let our arm be strong.

This for our own sake. For the sake of mankind, if this war brings home to us that we now sit in the council of nations and share directly in the general responsibility for the world's well-being, we shall have taken a great stride in national and spiritual maturity, and our talk about the brotherhood of man may progress from rhetoric towards realization.

XV

XV

W E have yet to find our greater selves. We have also yet to realize that Europe, since the Spanish War, has counted us in the concert of great nations far more than we have counted ourselves.

Somebody wrote in the New York Sun:

We are not English, German, Swede,
Or Austrian, Russian, French or Pole;
But we have made a separate breed
'   *And gained a separate soul.*

It sounds well; it means nothing; its sum total is zero. America asserts the

brotherhood of man and then talks about
a separate soul !

To speak of the Old World and the
New World is to speak in a dead language. The world is one. All humanity is in the same boat. The
passengers multiply, but the boat re-
mains the same size. And people who
rock the boat must be stopped by force.
America can no more separate itself
from the destiny of Europe than it can
escape the natural laws of the universe.

Because we declared political independence, does any one still harbor the
delusion that we are independent of the
acts and fortunes of monarchs? If so,
let him consider only these four events:
In 1492 a Spanish Queen financed a
sailor named Columbus — and Europe
reached out and laid a hand on this

hemisphere. In 1685 a French King
revoked an edict — and thousands of
Huguenots enriched our stock. In 1803
a French consul, to spite Britain, sold us
some land — it was pretty much everything west of the Mississippi. One
might well have supposed we were independent of the heir of Austria. In
1914 they killed him, and Europe fell
to pieces — and that fall is shaking
our ship of state from stem to stern.
There may be some citizens down in
the hold who do not know it — among a
hundred million people you cannot expect to have no imbeciles.

Thus, from Palos, in 1492, to Sarajevo,
in 1914, the hand of Europe has drawn
us ever and ever closer.

Yes, indeed; we are all in the same
boat. Europe has never forgotten some

words spoken here once: "That government of the people, by the people, for the people, shall not perish from the earth." She waited to hear us repeat that in some form when The Hague conventions we signed were torn to scraps of paper. Perhaps nothing save calamity will teach us what Europe is thankful to have learned again — that some things are worse than war, and that you can pay too high a price for peace; but that you cannot pay too high for the finding and keeping of your own soul.

[FINIS]

Printed in United States of America.